Karen's Christmas Tree

Other books by
Ann M. Martin

Leo The Magnificat
Rachel Parker, Kindergarten Show-off
Eleven Kids, One Summer
Ma and Pa Dracula
Yours Turly, Shirley
Ten Kids, No Pets
With You and Without You
Me and Katie (the Pest)
Stage Fright
Inside Out
Bummer Summer

THE BABY-SITTERS CLUB series
THE BABY-SITTERS CLUB mysteries
THE KIDS IN MS. COLMAN'S CLASS series
BABY-SITTERS LITTLE SISTER series
(see inside book covers for a complete listing)

BABY-SITTERS
Little Sister

Karen's Christmas Tree
Ann M. Martin

Illustrations by Susan Tang

A
LITTLE APPLE
PAPERBACK

SCHOLASTIC INC.
New York Toronto London Auckland Sydney

ISBN 0-590-69188-0

Copyright © 1996 by Ann M. Martin. All rights reserved. Published by Scholastic Inc. BABY-SITTERS LITTLE SISTER is a registered trademark of Scholastic Inc. LITTLE APPLE PAPERBACKS and the LITTLE APPLE PA-PERBACKS logo are trademarks of Scholastic Inc.

12 11 10 9 8 7 6 5 4 3 2 1   6 7 8 9/9 0 1/0

Printed in the U.S.A   40

First Scholastic printing, December 1996

*The author gratefully acknowledges
Stephanie Calmenson
for her help
with this book.*

Karen's Christmas Tree

The Holiday Spirit

"Who would like more tea?" I asked my friends.

"Just a drop for me," said Hannie.

I picked up the teapot to pour some pretend tea.

"Um, excuse me, but your necklace is in your teacup," I said, giggling.

Hannie and Nancy looked at the long string of pink beads hanging in Hannie's cup. They started giggling, too.

"I think my necklace is thirsty," said Hannie.

We were having a Lovely Ladies tea party in my room at the little house. We were dressed up in our best Lovely Ladies clothes.

I am Karen Brewer. I am seven years old. I have blonde hair, blue eyes, and a bunch of freckles. I am a glasses-wearer, too. I wear my blue pair for reading. I wear my pink pair the rest of the time.

Nancy Dawes and Hannie Papadakis are my two best friends. We call ourselves the Three Musketeers. That is because we like to do everything together. Our motto is "One for all and all for one!"

"Christmas is coming soon," I said. "I hope I will get some new clothes for my dolls."

"Hanukkah will be here before Christmas," said Nancy. "The thing I want most is to go to a play — a big, professional play."

"I heard an ad on the radio for *Annie*.

It is at a theater in Stamford," said Hannie.

We live in Stoneybrook, Connecticut. Stamford is not too far away.

"Tickets to those plays cost a lot of money. Wouldn't you rather have doll clothes?" I asked.

"No way. You know I would like to be an actress someday," said Nancy. "I need to see a lot of plays."

Knock, knock.

"Who is it?" I asked.

"Me," said a voice. It was Andrew's voice. Andrew is my little brother. He is four going on five.

"Come in," I replied.

Andrew came in holding a piece of paper.

"I want to draw a picture to bring to school tomorrow," said Andrew. "I want to draw Santa and his sled. I forgot how many reindeer Santa has."

My friends and I tried our best not to laugh at Andrew's picture. We could not see

Santa or his sled anywhere. All we saw were scribbles.

"Santa has eight reindeer," I said.

"Dasher, Dancer, and Prancer," said Hannie.

"Vixen, Comet, and Cupid," said Nancy.

"And do not forget Donner and Blitzen," I added.

"I do not have room for eight reindeer," said Andrew. He looked worried.

"Then draw two reindeer and say the rest ran off the paper," I said.

Andrew's face lit up. "Thank you!" he said. He ran back to his room to finish his drawing.

Ding-dong!

I wondered who was at the door. A minute later I found out.

"The pizza is here!" called Mommy.

"We will be right down," I replied.

My friends and I were having a middle-of-the-week pizza party! It was only the beginning of December. But my family was already getting into the holiday spirit.

I wondered if my other family at the big house were getting into the holiday spirit, too. Wait. I have not told you yet about my two houses and two families. I better do that right now.

2

Not One But Two

This is the story of why I have not one but two of so many things. It starts when I was little.

Way back then, I lived in one big house with Mommy, Daddy, and Andrew. But then Mommy and Daddy started to fight. They could not work things out, even though they tried. Mommy and Daddy explained to Andrew and me that they loved us very much. But they could not get along with each other, so they got a divorce.

Mommy moved with Andrew and me to a little house not too far away in Stoneybrook, Connecticut. Then she met a man named Seth and married him. That is how Seth became my stepfather. So the people at the little house are Mommy, Seth, Andrew, and me. The pets are Midgie, Seth's dog; Rocky, Seth's cat; Emily Junior, my pet rat; and Bob, Andrew's hermit crab.

Daddy stayed at the big house after the divorce. (It is the house he grew up in.) Then he met Elizabeth. Daddy married Elizabeth. That is how Elizabeth became my stepmother and I got a second family. A big one. Elizabeth was married once before and has four children. They are my stepbrothers and stepsister. They are David Michael, who is seven like me; Kristy, who is thirteen and the best stepsister ever; and Sam and Charlie, who are so old they are in high school.

I have another sister, Emily Michelle. Emily is two and a half. She was adopted from a faraway country called Vietnam. I love her a lot. That is why I named my special rat after her.

Another important person lives at the big house. That person is Nannie. She is Elizabeth's mother, which means she is my stepgrandmother. She helps take care of everyone.

There are also pets at the big house. They are Shannon, David Michael's big Bernese mountain dog puppy; Boo-Boo, Daddy's cranky old cat; Crystal Light the Second, my goldfish; and Goldfishie, Andrew's reindeer. (Just kidding!)

Andrew and I switch houses every month — one month we live at the little house, the next month at the big house. Sometimes we stay at one house for two months in a row. For example, we are going to be at the little house in December *and* January this year.

I gave Andrew and me special names. I call us Andrew Two-Two and Karen Two-Two. (I thought up those names after my teacher read a book to our class. It was called *Jacob Two-Two Meets the Hooded Fang*.)

I call us those names because we have two of so many things. Having two sets of things makes switching houses a lot easier.

We each have two sets of toys and clothes and books — one set at each house. I have two bicycles. Andrew has two tricycles. I have two stuffed cats. Goosie lives at the little house. Moosie lives at the big house. I have two pieces of Tickly, my special blanket. And you know I have two best friends. But I did not tell you that Nancy lives right next door to the little house. And Hannie lives across the street and one house down from the big house.

So that is how I got to have not one but *two* houses, *two* families, *two* best friends, and *two* of so many things!

3

The Wish Tree

On Saturday morning Seth made blueberry pancakes for breakfast. While we were eating, we decided to start thinking about Christmas decorations.

"How about having a special project this year?" said Seth. "We could each make an ornament for the tree."

"Cool!" said Andrew and I at the exact same time.

I think we were excited about making Christmas ornaments because last year we had an ornament disaster. We were going to buy an angel for the tree at the big house. Then we dropped it in the store and broke it. At the last minute we had to fix up a raggedy pipe-cleaner angel I had made at school and put it on top of the tree.

"Making ornaments is a wonderful idea," said Mommy. "We have to run some errands downtown this morning anyway. We can stop at the crafts store while we are there and pick up the things we need."

"Yippee!" I said.

After breakfast we cleaned up, then piled into the car and headed downtown.

"This year I am going to make a really beautiful angel for our tree," I said.

"I am going to make reindeer," said Andrew. "I will make eight of them. I will hang them all around the tree."

When we got downtown, we were lucky to find a parking spot right away. And it was just a few doors from the Unicorn Toy Store.

"May we look at the toys in the window?" I asked.

"Yes, but quickly. We have a lot to do this morning," replied Mommy.

Andrew and I raced to the toy store. In one window a toy train was running on its tracks. In the other were dolls, cars, trucks, and stuffed animals.

"Look, they have a tree inside," said Andrew.

He pointed to a Christmas tree just inside the store. It was decorated in an unusual way. Instead of tinsel and ordinary Christmas ornaments, paper stars were hanging from it. I could see words written on the stars, but I was too far away to read them.

"We are going inside just for a minute," I called to Mommy and Seth. They were looking at some antiques in the window next door. We hurried into the toy store before they could say no.

A clerk was by the tree, hanging up a few more stars.

"What do the stars say?" I asked.

"This is our Wish Tree," replied the clerk. "On each star is written the wish of a local

child who is not likely to receive any holiday gifts this year. Anyone who is interested may take one of the stars and grant a wish. Any toy sold to grant a wish is sold at a special discount. Our goal is to *undec*orate this tree before the holidays are over."

Wow. It *was* an unusual tree. I wondered what some of the wishes were. I was about to read some when Seth poked his head in the door.

"Karen and Andrew, it is time to go," he said.

"Okay," I replied.

"Anyone can grant a wish," the clerk called after us. "Think about it."

I could hardly think of anything else the rest of the morning. I thought about the Wish Tree while we were at the crafts store. I thought about it while we were at the hardware store. I thought about it while we were eating lunch.

I was still thinking about it on the ride home. I decided that thinking was not enough. I had to *do* something.

4

A Three-Star Day

The first thing I did was call my friends. I told each of them about the special tree.

"We need to have a Three Musketeers meeting," I told Hannie, then Nancy.

Hannie's father drove Hannie to my house. Nancy ran over from next door. We went straight to my room.

"Let's take a vote," I said. "Who would like to grant a wish?"

"I would like to, but it will not be easy," said Hannie. "I have started saving my allowance already, and I still think I might have trouble buying gifts for my family and my friends."

"Me too," said Nancy. "But I want to grant a wish also. Maybe we could make some of the gifts instead of buying them. And we could do chores to earn some money."

"Then we can put all our money together. I am sure the three of us will have enough money to grant one wish," I said. "All in favor say aye!"

"Aye!" said the Three Musketeers.

We wanted to go to the toy store right away to pick our star. Mommy and Seth did not have time to drive us. Luckily Nancy's father was not too busy and was happy to take us.

As soon as the clerk saw me walk back into the toy store, a big smile spread across his face.

"I was hoping I would see you again," he said.

We told the clerk what we wanted to do.

"So the three of you want to grant one

wish," said the clerk. "That is an excellent idea."

"It cannot be too expensive," I added.

"One not-too-expensive wish coming right up," said the clerk.

He read a few of the wishes, then took one down from the tree. He held the Wish Tree star up for us to read.

It said:

Fire truck, please.
Martin

It was perfect.

The clerk took our names and phone numbers.

"We need the toy here the week before Christmas," he said.

"No problem!" said Nancy.

"See you soon," said Hannie.

"Don't go yet," said the clerk. "I will be right back."

He ran to the back of the store. When he returned, he was holding two more stars.

18

He had written the same wish on each one.

"Everyone granting a wish needs a star to keep her going," he said.

"Thank you!" we replied.

We headed out of the store with stars in hand. I felt gigundoly proud. I could hardly wait to grant my Wish Tree wish.

Nancy's News

On Tuesday morning I was at the back of my classroom talking with Hannie and Nancy. Our teacher, Ms. Colman, had not arrived yet. Nancy had exciting news. She had already told me on the bus. Now she was telling Hannie.

"Remember the advertisement you heard for *Annie*?" asked Nancy. "Well, guess who has tickets? Me!"

"Cool!" said Hannie. "Where did the tickets come from?"

"Grandma B sent them to me for a Hanukkah present," replied Nancy.

Grandma B is Nancy's adopted Grandma. She lives at Stoneybrook Manor. That is a place where old people live when they cannot take care of themselves very easily anymore.

"The show is at a special children's theater. Kids can go by themselves without a grown-up. I have two tickets so I can take a friend," said Nancy.

"When is the show?" I asked.

"It is a week from Friday," replied Nancy.

"Oh, bullfrogs. I think that is the night Andrew's school puts on its holiday festival," I said.

Just then Ms. Colman walked into the classroom.

"Good morning, class," she said. "Everyone, please take your seats."

"See you later," I said to my friends.

My seat is at the front of the room. I used to sit at the back with Hannie and Nancy. But when I got my glasses, Ms. Colman moved me up front so I could see better.

I am not the only glasses-wearer in the room. Natalie Springer wears glasses. Ricky Torres wears glasses, too. (Ricky is my pretend husband. We got married on the playground at recess one day.) We sit in the front row together. Oh, one more person is a glasses-wearer. Ms. Colman!

"Karen, would you like to take attendance this morning?" asked Ms. Colman.

"Sure!" I replied. I love when I get to take attendance. I do it quickly and I never make a mistake.

I decided to do it faster than I ever did it before. I looked at the clock on the wall. It said five minutes after nine. When the big hand reached the twelve, I began.

I quickly put five checks in the book, for me, Hannie, Nancy, Natalie, and Ricky. I looked around the room. I saw Addie Sidney. She was doodling on her wheelchair tray. (She uses a wipe-off marker.) Check for Addie. I saw Pamela Harding. (She is my best enemy.) Check. Pamela was whispering to her buddies, Jannie Gilbert and Leslie Morris. Check, check. I saw Terri and Tammy Barkan, who are twins. Two more checks. Audrey Green was there. Check. Sara Ford was there. Check. Hank Reubens, Omar Harris, Bobby Gianelli, and Chris Lamar were there. Check, check, check, check. I put a few more checks in the book. Then I handed it back to Ms. Colman and looked at the clock. It was only eight minutes after nine. That had to be an attendance-taking record.

"Thank you, Karen," said Ms. Colman. "That was very fast."

"You are welcome!" I replied.

Did I tell you yet that Ms. Colman is a gigundoly wonderful teacher? Well, she is. Some teachers would notice how fast I took the attendance, but would not say anything. Ms. Colman always says nice things. And she never, ever yells at us. (Sometimes she has to remind me to use my indoor voice when I get excited and shout in class. But she always does it nicely.)

23

"We are going to start with spelling," said Ms. Colman. "Please take out your workbooks."

All right! Spelling happens to be one of my favorite subjects. This was a very good way to start the day.

6

Wish Tree Chores

Nancy and I walked home from the bus together after school.

"Hi, Mr. Drucker! Hi, Mrs. Drucker!" we called.

Our neighbors, Mr. and Mrs. Drucker, were coming home with some groceries. They are a very nice older couple. Mr. Drucker is in a garden club called the Green Thumbs. Once on St. Patrick's Day I got to ride in the Green Thumbs' parade float.

The Druckers waved to us. But they looked kind of sad. Nancy and I wondered if anything were wrong. Maybe one of them was not feeling well. Then Mommy would make some soup and I could take it to them.

Nancy and I looked both ways, then crossed the street.

"Hello, girls. How are you today?" asked Mr. Drucker.

"We are fine. How are you? You do not look so happy," I replied. (I did not know if I was supposed to say that. But it was the truth.)

Mrs. Drucker smiled a sad smile.

"You are right," she said. "We are sad that we lost our beautiful blue-spruce tree this summer. It was so hot and dry, our tree could not survive."

I looked at the place where the tree used to stand.

"It *is* sad," I replied. "That was the tree you always decorated for Christmas. It made the whole street look pretty."

"We will have to do without it this year. We will put lights on our house and have

candles in our windows instead," said Mr. Drucker.

"Would the two of you like to come inside for some cider?" asked Mrs. Drucker.

"Thank you, but I have chores to do today," said Nancy.

"Me too," I replied. "Thank you anyway."

Nancy and I looked both ways, then carefully crossed back to our side of the street. I really would miss the Druckers' tree. It was fun to look out my living-room window and see it all dressed up for the holidays.

I said good-bye to Nancy. There was no time for us to play. We each had Wish Tree chores to do.

I started my chores right after my snack with Andrew.

First I helped Mommy wash and dry Christmas cookie tins. We sang Christmas songs while we worked.

"Sleigh bells ring! Are you listenin'? In the lane, snow is glistenin'!"

When we finished, Mommy gave me a quarter.

My next chore was to count a stack of Christmas cards left over from last year. That way Mommy and Seth would know how many new cards they needed to buy.

"Twenty-three cards and twenty-four envelopes," I said.

"Thank you," said Mommy. She handed me a dime.

I read "The Night Before Christmas" to Andrew. The poem was in a picture book. Andrew asked me to read it three times. Mommy gave me another dime. (I usually read to Andrew for free. But Mommy said she was happy to pay me because the money was going to a good cause.)

I helped Mommy cook dinner. I helped Seth clean up. They each gave me two dimes and a nickel.

"May I have this container?" I asked Seth. I held up one of the small plastic containers we had just washed and dried.

"It is all yours," said Seth.

"Thanks," I replied.

I took the container up to my room. I covered it with green paper. I taped the red Wish Star on the front. Then I dropped in the money I had earned. One quarter. Six dimes. Two nickels.

That made ninety-five cents. Not bad for my first day on the job.

7

A Very Good Plan

On Wednesday morning I was cozy in bed when I heard sirens wailing outside my window. At first I thought I was dreaming. Then I opened my eyes. I did not hear sirens anymore. I heard car doors slamming and people talking.

I jumped out of bed and ran to my window. An ambulance was parked in the Druckers' driveway. The ambulance workers were putting a stretcher into the back. Seth was there, talking to Mr. Drucker. I did not see Mrs. Drucker. I ran downstairs.

"Mommy, what is wrong with Mrs. Drucker?" I asked.

Mommy put her arm around me.

"I do not know yet. Seth went over to help out. He will be able to tell us what happened to Mrs. Drucker," Mommy said.

In a few minutes Seth returned.

"How is Mrs. Drucker? What happened to her?" I asked.

"Mrs. Drucker fell earlier this morning. The medical workers think she broke her hip," Seth replied. "They expect her to be in the hospital for about three weeks."

"That is a long time," I said. "When I broke my wrist, the doctor at the hospital fixed me up and sent me right home the same day."

"A broken hip is more serious than a broken wrist," said Mommy. "Also, things take more time to heal when a person is older."

I started to feel sad. And worried. I have friends who have gone into the hospital. Nancy. Bobby. They came out just fine. But the last old person I knew who went into the hospital was my grandad. And he died.

"Will Mrs. Drucker really be all right? Will she really come home in three weeks?" I asked.

"Yes, Karen," said Seth. "You might be thinking about Grandad now. But he was very, very ill. These days a broken hip can be fixed."

"I will call the hospital later and find out how Mrs. Drucker is doing," said Mommy. "Right now it is time to get ready for school."

I woke Andrew up. He had slept through the commotion. I got dressed, ate some breakfast, and made it to the school bus just in time. Nancy had saved me a seat.

"Did you see them take Mrs. Drucker away in the ambulance this morning?" I asked.

"I sure did. The sirens woke me up," replied Nancy.

"The Druckers are so nice. We should do something special to cheer them up," I said.

"We could make get-well cards for Mrs.

Drucker," said Nancy. "And send her some balloons."

Those were both good ideas. But I did not think they were special enough for Mrs. Drucker. I thought hard.

"I know! Mr. and Mrs. Drucker were really sad about not having their tree. We could get them a new one. That would cheer them up," I said.

"That is a great idea!" said Nancy. "But wait. Don't trees like that cost a lot of money? We are already doing chores to get Wish Tree money."

"You are right. We need help," I replied. "We can ask our neighbors if they will chip in. We can buy a real live tree at the nursery. We can put it right in the spot where the old tree used to stand. It will be a surprise."

"Won't Mr. Drucker see us putting it there?" asked Nancy.

"We will find out when Mrs. Drucker is coming home. Then when Mr. Drucker goes to pick her up, we will bring over the tree.

34

It will be the first thing they see when they come home," I said.

"They will be so surprised!" said Nancy.

"And so happy!" I said.

Nancy and I were happy already. This was a very good plan.

8

Two Against One

When we reached school, Nancy raced to her desk. I thought she was hurrying to tell Hannie about Mrs. Drucker and our plan. But the first thing she said was "Hannie, did you ask your mom and dad?"

I wondered what she was talking about.

"Yes, and they said I can go!" Hannie replied.

That made me even more curious.

"Go where?" I asked.

"Nancy asked me to go to *Annie* with her," replied Hannie.

I turned to Nancy and glared. I could hardly believe it.

"Why didn't you ask *me*?" I asked.

Nancy looked surprised. "You said you could not go," she replied.

"Well, it just so happens I *can* go. Andrew's school festival is being held on Thursday, not Friday. I mixed up the dates a little, that's all," I said. "Anyway, it would have been nice to have been asked."

"How was I supposed to know you mixed up the dates?" said Nancy.

"You were supposed to ask me to the play!" I replied. "Then you would have found out."

I stomped off to my desk. Nancy followed me.

"If you don't mind, I would like to be left alone," I said. "I would rather be alone than with someone like you. You are selfish and mean and I do not want to be your friend anymore!"

I expected Nancy to say something mean back to me. But she did not. She started to

cry. I watched her run back to her desk and start talking to Hannie. She must have been telling Hannie what I said. The next thing I knew Hannie was stomping over to my desk.

"I already explained to Nancy that I want to be alone," I said.

"I just came to tell you that you did not have to be so mean," said Hannie. "Nancy did not do anything wrong. She thought you could not go to the play. That is why she asked me instead of you."

"She did not waste any time asking you," I replied. "And she did not seem one bit sorry that I could not go. Even if it was true. Which it is not."

"It is not her fault. She is not being mean. You are," said Hannie. She stomped back to her desk.

I sat at my desk by myself. I watched Hannie and Nancy sitting together. It was two against one. That made me madder than ever.

9

Not Invited

When Ms. Colman came in, she asked Hannie to take attendance. Boo. Hannie gave me a meanie-mo look. I gave her one right back.

Hannie needed a lot longer to take attendance than I had. When she finally finished, Ms. Colman said, "We are going to have a spelling quiz this morning, class. I hope you studied your word list last night."

I had studied very well. I knew every word perfectly. Ms. Colman went around the room asking each of us to spell a word. My word was *separate*.

"That is easy," I said. "There is a rat in the middle of *separate*. S-e-p-a-r-a-t-e."

I looked at Nancy when I got to r-a-t. Nancy looked up at the ceiling.

Hannie's spelling word was *believe*.

"B-E-L-E-I-V-E," said Hannie.

Ha! Hannie spelled the word wrong. I was glad. I waved my hand in the air and Ms. Colman called on me.

"B-E-L-I-E-V-E," I said.

"Very good, Karen. Hannie, I am sure you will get it right the next time," said Ms. Colman.

I turned to give Hannie a know-it-all look. She looked down at the floor.

The rest of the morning went slowly. I usually turn around a few times and wave to Hannie and Nancy at the back of the room. Sometimes we make funny faces or hold up notes. But I did not turn around even once.

At lunchtime I made sure to sit as far

away from Hannie and Nancy as I could. I sat with Natalie so I would not be alone. I ended up alone half the time anyway. That is because Natalie kept disappearing under the table to pull up her socks. (Natalie's socks are always drooping.)

When we went out to the playground at recess, Hannie and Nancy ran to the monkey bars. They climbed to the top and sat there talking and giggling. They did not invite me to join them.

I tried to act as though I was having a great time jumping rope with Natalie. But she kept tripping on the rope, then starting over. I had to wait forever for my turn.

I watched Hannie and Nancy climb down from the monkey bars. They played hopscotch next. I felt like playing hopscotch, too. I had even brought my lucky hopscotch stone. But they did not invite me to join them.

I did not like this two-against-one fight at all. I did not think it would last long,

though. I was sure it would be over by the end of the day.

The bell rang to let us know recess was over. Hannie and Nancy walked into the room holding hands. They did not invite me to join them.

10

Waiting

In the afternoon Mr. Mackey, the art teacher, wheeled in the art cart. If anything can cheer me up, it is arts and crafts.

"Good afternoon, everyone," said Mr. Mackey. "I thought you might want to start making holiday decorations for your classroom. I brought extra red, green, gold, blue, and silver supplies."

All right!

Nancy got to help pass some of the supplies around. When she reached my row, she asked Natalie and Ricky what colors they wanted. But she did not say one word to me. She pointed at the supplies. I took the ones I wanted. I did not say thank you.

I did not say a word to my ex-friends all afternoon. They did not say a word to me. When the bell rang at the end of the day, our fight was still going on.

It was still going on when Nancy and I boarded the school bus. Nancy waited until I got on and sat down. Then she got on the bus and sat down in another row. (I wished I had done that first!)

When we got off the bus, we walked in single file down our street.

I did not think the fight would go on much longer. My ex-friends would probably call me that afternoon to make up.

"How was school today?" asked Mommy when I walked through the front door.

"It was fine," I said. "I did well on my spelling quiz. And we started making decorations for our room."

I did not tell her about the fight. Why

bother, when it was going to be over any minute?

"Andrew is at a friend's house this afternoon. Would you like to go to the supermarket with me?" asked Mommy.

"Sure! I mean . . . no, thank you," I replied. "I have homework to do."

I love going to the supermarket. I am an excellent shopping-cart pusher. But I did not want to be out when Hannie and Nancy called. That is why I said I had to do my homework.

"All right," said Mommy. "I will ask Seth to stop at the market on his way home from work."

I went to my room and flopped onto my bed. I picked up Goosie.

"You are not mad at me, are you?" I asked.

I made Goosie shake his head.

"Thanks, Goosie," I said. Whenever I was feeling blue, Goosie made me feel better.

Ring, ring! Hooray! I tried to guess if the phone call was from Nancy or Hannie. I waited for Mommy to call *Karen! Telephone!*

She did not. I pretended the phone rang again. This time it was for me.

"Ring, ring! Hi, Karen. This is Nancy," I said to Goosie. "I just want to tell you how sorry I am that I did not invite you to see *Annie* with me. It was very wrong. Can you ever forgive me?"

I decided to forgive her right away. That is because I am such a good friend. When I finished my pretend conversation with Nancy, I had a pretend conversation with Hannie. I forgave her, too.

When I finished my pretend conversations, I tried to do my homework. But I could not concentrate. I was too busy listening for the phone.

The afternoon was boring. And lonely.

I was still waiting for the phone to ring when I got into bed and turned out the light.

"Oh well, Goosie," I said. "I am not too worried. Tomorrow our fight will be over for sure."

Karen's Worries

On Thursday morning our class broke into reading groups. I was heading for the mystery group, but Hannie and Nancy got there first. I went to the biography group instead.

"I am surprised, Karen," said Ms. Colman. "I thought you would want to finish the mystery story you started reading last week."

"I decided it was boring," I said. "I would rather read a biography." (I knew I was fibbing. But why tell Ms. Colman about the fight when it was going to be over any minute?)

The fight was not over by lunchtime. I ate alone in the cafeteria. I was not in the mood to sit with Natalie again. And I felt too gloomy to sit with anyone else.

"Why aren't you sitting with your best friends?" asked Pamela, grinning. (Now you know why she is my best enemy.)

"I feel like sitting by myself today," I replied. "I have serious thinking to do."

"It looks more like serious fighting to me. Oh, well. Some friends just get along better than others," she said. And she skipped off to her table to join Jannie and Leslie.

I did not like people noticing our fight. I thought about hanging around with Hannie and Nancy on the playground. But I did not want them to think I forgave them when I did not.

So the fight went on. Hannie and Nancy climbed the monkey bars and I went on the swings all by myself.

When we returned to class in the afternoon, I did not turn around at all. Not even to make meanie-mo faces. That is because I was feeling gloomier by the minute. I was afraid if I turned around I might start to cry.

The fight was still going on when the school bell rang at the end of the day.

I let Nancy get on the bus first. Then I found a seat far away from her. I did not have much else to do on the ride home, so I started to worry. I worried that if my friends and I did not make up, it would be the end of the Three Musketeers. What would I call one friend all by herself? Lonely.

Then I found a new worry. I worried about our holiday plans. What would we do about the Wish Tree? What would we do about the Druckers' new blue-spruce tree? What would we do about giving holiday presents to each other? We always exchanged presents on a Saturday between Hanukkah and Christmas. I had even picked out their presents. I had gotten an excellent book for Nancy at a library sale. It

was about acting. I had gotten Hannie a book, too. It was a book of funny stories and poems. And I had gotten us three matching barrettes to wear together. (I decided it was okay to get a holiday gift for myself, too.)

The more I thought, the more miserable I felt. The holidays were coming and instead of having two good friends to celebrate with, I had two ex-friends who were not talking to me.

Boo-hoo-hoo and bullfrogs.

Ring, Ring

By dinnertime I was so miserable, I could hardly eat. We were having one of my favorite meals, too. Meatballs, spaghetti, and salad.

"You did not eat any of your snack, either," said Mommy. "Are you feeling all right?"

She put her hand on my forehead to see if I had a temperature.

"I am not sick," I said.

"Is there anything you would like to talk

about? You seem awfully blue lately," said Seth.

"My teacher read us a story about a blue kangaroo today," said Andrew. "It had pink spots because it had measles." He thought this was hysterically funny.

"May I please be excused?" I said. I wanted to go to my room.

"Yes, you may," replied Mommy. "If you get hungry later, just let me know. I will make you a snack."

"Thank you," I said.

I went to my room and spilled my Wish Tree money onto my bed. I had done lots more chores. Now I had $4.10. My friends — I mean ex-friends — and I had figured out that each of us needed to earn four dollars to buy the fire truck. I had all the money I needed. But I did not know what to do with it. I put the money back into my Wish Tree container.

Then I went to my closet and dug out the presents I had hidden there. I found the two books and the little bag with the barrettes. I felt like doing something useful. So I wrapped the presents. I made holiday gift wrapping out of construction paper. I drew Hanukkah candles on Nancy's paper and Christmas stars on Hannie's. When I finished, the packages looked beautiful. But I did not know what to do with them, either. I put them back in the closet.

I could not think of anything else that needed to be done. I looked out my window. Mr. Drucker must have been at the hospital. There were no lights on in the house and the yard was dark. I thought about calling the hospital to say hello to Mrs. Drucker. But I did not want to wake her if she was sleeping.

I did not think Hannie would be sleeping yet. Or Nancy. Hmm. Maybe it was time for me to call them.

I did not want anyone to know what I was doing. I tiptoed out of my room to the phone downstairs. I guess I did not tiptoe very softly.

"Karen, is that you?" called Mommy from the den. "Are you hungry? Would you like a snack?"

"No, thank you. I am just getting a glass of water," I replied.

I poured myself a glass of water and drank it so I would not be fibbing. Then I dialed Hannie's number.

Ring, ring! The phone rang twice. Then someone said, "Hello?"

It sounded like Linny, Hannie's brother. As soon as I heard his voice, I hung up. I was too scared to say anything. I dialed Nancy's number next.

Ring, ring, ring! The phone rang three times before someone picked up.

"Hello?" said a voice. It was Nancy! I hung up right away.

I would have liked to have talked to my friends. But I only had *ex*-friends, and I did not know what to say to them.

13

Three Wishes

At school the next morning, Ms. Colman handed out paper and gave us a special writing assignment.

"I would like you to write a short composition about a holiday wish," said Ms. Colman. "I would like to know what each of you wishes for most for Hanukkah, Christmas, or Kwanzaa."

I had a lot of wishes this year. The truth is I have a lot of wishes every year. I always wish for new toys and doll clothes because they are fun to have. I always wish for "no guns" because guns are dangerous and hurt and kill people.

I had the same wishes this year, but I also had two special wishes. I wished Mrs. Drucker would get well and come home soon. Mommy visited Mrs. Drucker at the hospital. She said Mrs. Drucker was getting better every day. So my first special wish was already working.

My other special wish was not working as well. I wished that my fight with Hannie and Nancy were over. I picked up my pencil and began to write. Ms. Colman had said to write a short composition. But I had a lot to say. Besides, I wanted Ms. Colman to know everything about our fight. Maybe she could help us end it, since we were having a hard time ending it on our own.

I wrote at the top of my paper, *My Christmas Wish*. Below that I wrote in big letters so Ms. Colman could not miss it, "I WISH MY FIGHT WITH MY TWO BEST FRIENDS WAS OVER." Then, as fast as I could, I wrote the story of what happened. And I wrote about how miserable I felt. (Even though I am an excellent speller, I was not sure how to spell *miserable*. So I wrote that I felt bad.)

"Class, it is time to finish up your compositions," said Ms. Colman. "Karen, would you like to collect them?"

Uh-oh. I still had a few more things to write. But I did not want to miss a chance to do an important job.

"If you need a couple more minutes, I can ask someone else to collect the papers," said Ms. Colman.

"No, I am done!" I replied.

I quickly scribbled "The end" at the bottom of my paper. I jumped out of my seat before Ms. Colman could ask someone else to collect the papers.

I started at the front of the room and worked my way back. Hannie's and Nancy's papers were the last two I collected. On my way to the front of the room, I took a peek at Nancy's wish. It said, "I wish my fight with my best friend, Karen, was over." I smiled to myself. Nancy's wish was the same as mine.

I peeked at Hannie's paper. She had the same wish.

I breathed a sigh of relief. My friends wanted to make up as much as I did. Now all we had to do was figure out how.

14

Talking Again

After school, it was my turn to get on the bus first. Nancy waited, then found a seat in another row. Without planning it, we had started taking turns getting on the bus first. One day I was first. The next day Nancy was.

Whoever got on first, got off last. I watched Nancy hop off the bus and run down the street. I followed slowly. Then Nancy stopped to check her mailbox and I caught up with her.

I love getting the mail in December. You

never know what will pop out of the box. Christmas cards. Gifts. An elephant . . .

Only none of those things was in the box. There were bills, advertisements, and more bills.

"Hello, girls!" called Mr. Drucker from across the street. "How are you doing today?"

"Fine!" I called back.

"Me too!" called Nancy. "How is Mrs. Drucker?"

"Is she coming home soon?" I called.

"She will be home a week from Saturday!" replied Mr. Drucker. "That is almost a week earlier than the doctors expected. She is doing very well."

"Say hello to her from me," said Nancy.

"Me too!" I called.

Mr. Drucker had a great big smile on his face. I had never seen him look happier.

"Thank you, girls. And thank you for the beautiful get-well cards," said Mr. Drucker. "See you later."

Hmm. I had made a get-well card for

Mrs. Drucker. I did not know Nancy had made one, too. I looked her way. When I saw Nancy looking back at me, I looked away again.

Then I started thinking. In just nine days Mrs. Drucker would be home. That meant we had only nine days to get the tree if we wanted it for a welcome-home surprise.

I looked at Nancy again. She was looking at me again.

"Well, if we are going to collect money for the tree, we better get started right away," I said.

"I know. I was thinking the same thing," replied Nancy.

"Maybe we could start collecting this afternoon. I'll ask and then call you, okay?"

"Okay. Talk to you later," said Nancy. " 'Bye."

Nancy ran into her house. I ran into mine. Neither of us had apologized. But at least we were talking. I felt a little bit better than before.

15

Apologies

Mommy said I could collect money from the neighbors if I followed a few rules. I could go only to the homes of people I knew well. I could ring the bell only once. I could ask only one time. (No nagging or begging.) I had to be home before dark. Nancy and I had to stick together.

I called Nancy right away.

"Can you go?" I asked.

"Yes, but I have a few rules to follow," replied Nancy.

They were almost exactly the same as

mine. We met in front of my house and started down the block. We rang the bells at our friends' houses first.

Ding-dong!

"Hi, Mr. Gianelli!" we said.

"Hello, Karen. Hello, Nancy. Bobby isn't home right now," said Mr. Gianelli.

"That is okay. We are not here to see Bobby. We would like to talk to you," I said. "We are trying to raise money to buy a new blue-spruce tree for the Druckers. Their tree died this summer and Mrs. Drucker is in the hospital."

"A new tree would cheer them up so much," said Nancy.

"I would be happy to help," said Mr. Gianelli.

He reached into his pocket and counted out his one dollar bills. There were a lot. He dropped them all into the small canvas bag Nancy's mother had given to us.

"Thank you, Mr. Gianelli!" said Nancy and I.

We rang the bell at Kathryn and Willie

Barnes's house next. Mrs. Barnes answered the door. Kathryn, who is six, and Willie, who is five, were right behind her.

"We are collecting money for a good cause," I said.

Nancy told the story of the Druckers and their tree.

"I will be right back," said Mrs. Barnes.

"Me too," said Kathryn. She ran off, with Willie following behind.

Mrs. Barnes came back with her wallet. Kathryn and Willie came back with their piggy banks. They all dropped money into the bag.

"Thank you!" said Nancy and I together again.

So far we were doing great. The Bartons' house was next. The Bartons are the newest family on the street. The kids are Jackie, who is seven; Lynda, who is eight; Meghan, who is four; Eric, who is ten; and Mark, who is twelve. Everyone made a contribution.

"Wait," said Mrs. Barton. "I have an idea."

She went away and came back with a string of holiday lights and a bag of tinsel.

"You can use these to decorate the Druckers' new tree," said Mrs. Barton.

"What a great idea!" I said.

"It is so nice that you are doing this together," said Mr. Barton. "You two must be very good friends."

Nancy and I looked at each other. After days of not talking, we did not feel like such good friends anymore.

We went to a few more houses. Our neighbors were very generous. A few more people commented on what wonderful friends Nancy and I seemed to be. I could not stand it any longer. I wanted us to be wonderful friends again.

"I am sorry I made you cry the other day," I said.

Nancy smiled at me. "I am sure you did not mean to," she said. "I am sorry I ganged up on you with Hannie."

"It's okay," I replied. Suddenly it did not

matter. "I think we better go home now. It is starting to get dark."

When we walked into the house, Mommy said she was proud of us for following all the rules and for collecting so much our first time out. She offered to help us count the money, but we told her we needed to make a phone call first.

We hurried to call Hannie.

"Guess what!" Nancy and I said into the phone together. "We made up!"

Nancy let me talk to Hannie myself. I apologized for being a meanie-mo. Hannie apologized too. The Three Musketeers' fight was finally over. Hooray!

Being Grown-up

I woke up the next morning with a very grown-up idea in my head. I think I must have dreamed it. I could hardly wait to get to school to tell Hannie and Nancy about it.

Nancy and I sat together on the bus. But I did not tell her my idea then. I wanted to tell my friends together.

I was happy Hannie was in the classroom when we arrived. I could not wait another minute to say what was on my mind.

I went to the back of the room with Nancy.

"Nancy and Hannie," I said, "I think it is wonderful that you will get to see *Annie* together. I hope you have a great time."

There. I had said it. Then I got a surprise. Hannie told me what was on *her* mind. It was very grown-up too.

"I do not think Nancy should take me to the play after all," said Hannie. "Choosing one friend out of two is too hard. I would not feel right going to the play knowing that you could have gone if I hadn't."

"But wait! I do not want to go instead of *you*," I replied.

"Hold everything!" said Nancy. "Isn't *anyone* going to go with me?"

"Someone will go with you. But it cannot be one of us," said Hannie. "You need to take somebody else."

"Who will Nancy take if it is not one of us?" I asked. "We are the most fun."

"Good morning, class," said Ms. Colman,

who had just arrived. "Please take your seats."

"See you at lunch," I said. "We will think of someone you can take to the play."

I had trouble keeping my mind on my schoolwork. I was too busy thinking about Nancy and her extra ticket. I looked around the room, trying to decide who Nancy would have fun with besides Hannie and me. I decided that no one would be as much fun as one of us. That is why we are the Three Musketeers.

I hoped we were not letting Nancy down. Maybe Hannie or I should go with her after all.

I did not have to worry. At lunchtime Nancy made an announcement.

"I know who to take," she said.

"Who?" asked Hannie and I together.

"I will take Grandma B!" replied Nancy. "Grandma B told me to take a friend. She is my friend. And she bought the tickets. We will go together."

"That is a great idea," said Hannie.

"It is perfect," I said. "You always have fun with Grandma B. And it will make her so happy to go with you."

That was it. Our problem was solved. I was gigundoly proud of the Three Musketeers for being so grown-up.

Giving Gifts

We went to Nancy's house after school.

"Are you girls hungry for a snack?" asked Mrs. Dawes.

"I am," said Nancy. "But I would like to make a phone call first. I want to call Grandma B."

Nancy's mother said she would make the snack while Nancy made her call. Hannie and I listened to every word.

"Hello, Grandma B. It's me, Nancy. I am calling to invite you out. I would like you to come see *Annie* with me. Will you, please?"

We watched a smile spread across Nancy's face. She gave us the thumbs-up sign. When she hung up, Nancy said she thought she had made Grandma B very happy. Yippee!

We ate our snack — melted cheese on toast and warm apple cider. Then the Three Musketeers got ready to make someone else happy.

Hannie already had her Wish Tree money with her. Nancy went up to her room to get hers. I ran next door to get mine. I also grabbed a roll of gift-wrapping paper. It had drummers, toy soldiers, and shining stars on it.

"We can wrap the gift while we are there," I said to my friends.

"Good idea," said Nancy.

Mrs. Dawes bundled up Nancy's baby brother, Danny. Then we piled into the car, buckled up, and rode to the Unicorn Toy

Store. It was time to buy our Wish Tree gift.

The store clerk smiled when he saw us.

"We have money to buy our gift," I said. "Could you please show us where the toy trucks are?"

The clerk pointed down an aisle at the back of the store.

"You'll find what you are looking for there," he said.

The Wish Tree star was still taped to my money container. I carefully took it off and reread Martin's wish.

Hannie walked over to a huge fire truck that kids could ride in. "I wish we could get this one for Martin," said she.

"I am sure we do not have enough money for that," I replied.

"How about this one?" asked Nancy.

She held up a small red plastic fire truck. It did not look too exciting.

Then I spotted a truck tucked away behind the rest. It was shiny. It came with a ladder. It was not too big or too small.

"If I were getting a fire truck, I would want this one," I said, carefully taking it from the shelf. I held it up to show my friends.

"That's the one!" said Nancy.

"How much does it cost?" asked Hannie.

We checked the price tag. With the discount we had just enough money to pay for it. *Ding, ding!* It even had a little bell.

We marched back to the front of the store.

"We would like to buy this fire truck," I said. "And if you would please give us scissors and tape, we will wrap it up ourselves."

"That is a fine truck," said the clerk. "You are going to make a child very happy on Christmas morning."

You know what? That made us happy, too.

18

The Most Special Tree

"Good morning, Goosie!" I said.

It was Saturday morning. I was up early because I was so excited. This was the Saturday that Mrs. Drucker was coming home!

Nancy and I had gone out a few more times to collect money for the Druckers' tree. Once Mommy came with us so we could go to houses that were a little farther away. We collected all the money we needed and enough lights to make the whole town of Stoneybrook glow!

I knew Mommy and Seth were already

up because I could hear them in the kitchen. I ran downstairs to say good morning.

"Why don't you call Nancy and invite her to join us for breakfast?" asked Seth.

"All right," I replied. "What are we having?"

"How about French toast?" said Seth.

I called Nancy right away. (I think I woke her dad.) Nancy said she would come over as soon as she got dressed.

We ate Seth's yummy French toast. Then Mommy drove Nancy and me to the nursery.

"Girls, I am going to let you pick out the tree yourselves. When you find one that you like, I will come see it," said Mommy.

Nancy and I looked at each other. This was a big responsibility. We were choosing the tree that our whole neighborhood had chipped in to buy.

"We picked a very good fire truck," I said. "I know we will pick a good tree, too."

Mommy sat down on a bench where she

could watch us and wait till we made our choice.

Uh-oh. Choosing a tree was not going to be as easy as choosing the fire truck. There were so many beautiful trees — tall trees, full trees, bluer trees, greener trees.

"We'd better look at the prices," said Nancy. "Some of these may be too expensive."

It was true. Some of the trees cost more money than we had. That made our job easier. But it was still hard.

Then, at almost the same time, we saw a very special tree off in a corner.

"It looks like the Druckers' old tree," said Nancy.

"It sure does," I said. "I bet they would like that."

We studied the tree. We studied it from top to bottom. We walked around and studied every side. We looked at the price tag.

"Let's check the other trees one more time," said Nancy.

We looked at the other trees, but none

was as special. We called to Mommy.

"This is the one!" I said, pointing to the tree. "What do you think?"

"It is a beauty!" Mommy replied. "It is full and healthy. And it looks a lot like the Druckers' old tree."

Nancy and I smiled. We had done our job very well.

We paid for the tree. Then two men who worked at the nursery tied it up and loaded it into the car. When we got home, we called everyone in our neighborhood. The plan was to meet at eleven o'clock sharp in the Druckers' front yard. We would decorate the tree together. (Mr. Drucker was already at the hospital.)

Seth and Mr. Gianelli carried the tree across the street to the Druckers' yard. We left it in the pot because the earth was too cold for planting.

By eleven o'clock all the neighbors had arrived.

"It is perfect!" said Mrs. Barton. "The Druckers will be very pleased."

We strung the lights and tinsel. Some neighbors brought ornaments, and we hung those, too. We were ready.

The Druckers would not be home until the evening. That is when Seth would light the tree. I could hardly wait.

19

Welcome Home!

Mommy had made friends with a nurse at the hospital. The nurse promised to call us when the Druckers left. It was late in the afternoon when the phone rang. Mommy answered it. When she hung up, she smiled.

"The Druckers are on their way home," she said.

We called all the neighbors again. This time the plan was for everyone to come over right away. We all gathered in the Druckers' yard.

I was thinking it would be fun to hide.

Then, when the Druckers arrived, we could all pop out and yell *Surprise!* But I decided that might be too scary. I was thinking of another plan when Seth called, "Here they come!"

I was so happy and excited, I could not stop jumping up and down. I was happy Mrs. Drucker was coming home. I was excited because I could not wait for them to see their new blue-spruce tree.

The sky was almost dark when the car drove into the driveway. Seth pulled a switch and lit the tree. By the glowing lights we could see the smiles on Mr. and Mrs. Drucker's faces. They looked as happy as I had ever seen them.

"Welcome home!" we all cried.

Mr. Drucker stepped out of the car. "Thank you, everyone," he said. "This is the best surprise we have ever had. Now if you wait just a moment, my wife would like to thank you, too."

Mr. Drucker went around to the back of the car. Everyone waited quietly — even me

— as Mr. Drucker took a walker out of the trunk. He carried it to Mrs. Drucker's side of the car, opened the door, and helped her out.

Mrs. Drucker looked tired, but very happy. I ran to her and threw my arms around her. (I was careful not to hurt her.)

"Welcome home!" I said.

"Thank you, Karen. Thank you, everyone," said Mrs. Drucker. "This is the most beautiful tree. In fact, it reminds me of our old tree that we loved so much."

"Karen and Nancy picked it out all by themselves," said Mommy.

I looked at Nancy and smiled. I felt gigundoly proud.

"We would like to visit with you all, but I'm afraid it's been a long and tiring day," said Mr. Drucker.

"We are very lucky tonight," added Mrs. Drucker. "We get to sit inside our house together and look at the beautiful tree our good neighbors gave us."

Mrs. Drucker started up her walk one

small step at a time. Mr. Drucker was on one side. I was on the other. Slowly, step by step, she reached her door.

Someone in the crowd started to clap very quietly. Another person joined in. Soon everyone was clapping for Mr. and Mrs. Drucker and their brand-new tree.

Then it was time for us to go. Mommy left the chicken soup she had made. Many of the neighbors had brought food and holiday baskets for the Druckers. We said our good nights and went back to our houses. It was a happy night for us all.

Trimming the Tree

The happy night was not over yet. After dinner Mommy said, "Who is ready to trim the tree?"

"Me!" Andrew and I shouted.

Seth had surprised us by bringing home our own tree on Wednesday. It was not as big as the Druckers' tree. But it was friendly with branches that spread out like open arms.

"I will be right back!" I called. "I am going to get my ornament."

"Me too," said Andrew.

I had worked hard on my ornament this year, and I had finished it on Tuesday.

I found the ornament, and Goosie, too.

"Come on, Goosie, let's go!" I said.

I carried Goosie downstairs and set him on the couch with the ornament on his lap. I had hidden the ornament in a paper bag.

Andrew came downstairs hiding his ornament behind him.

"You can go first," I said. "I will go last."

Sometimes it is fun to be last.

Andrew held out his ornament. It was some kind of paper animal. At first I thought it was a dog. Then I saw red scribbling on its nose.

"It is Rudolph the Red-Nosed Reindeer," I said.

"That's it!" said Andrew proudly.

"It is a wonderful ornament," said Mommy.

"It sure is," said Seth. "Come hang it on the tree."

Andrew hung his reindeer on a branch near the bottom.

"Karen, would you like your turn now?" asked Seth.

"I would like you and Mommy to go next," I replied.

Mommy showed us her ornament next. She had made a Santa out of pipe cleaners and colored foil.

"Ho, ho, ho!" said Mommy, laughing.

"Put him next to Rudolph," said Andrew.

Mommy hung her Santa Claus next to Andrew's reindeer.

"Now it is my turn," said Seth.

He held up a handsome toy soldier made out of wood. The soldier was holding a drum.

"Rum-pum-pum, rum-pum-pum," sang Seth.

"He is beautiful," said Mommy.

Andrew and I thought so too. Seth hung his soldier on the other side of the tree. Finally it was my turn. I took my package from Goosie's lap.

"Ta-daa!" I said. I held up a star made of clay. I had sprayed it with gold paint and put sparkles on it. It was very spangly.

"I love it," said Mommy.

"It is a wish star. I wrote a message on the back," I said. I turned it over for my family to see.

I WISH EVERYONE A VERY MERRY CHRISTMAS!

"I think your wish star would be the perfect ornament for the top of the tree," said Seth. "Does everyone agree?"

Everyone answered yes. Hooray! Seth got a ladder and held me as I set my star in the place of honor at the top of the tree. It looked right at home there.

We hung the rest of our ornaments, then added lights and tinsel. The happy night was almost over. But I had more happy things to look forward to. I had not had my holiday party with my friends yet. And Ms. Colman had promised we would have a holiday party at school, too. After that would come Christmas Day.

I looked out the window at the Druckers' glowing tree. Then I looked up at my wish star. I knew my wish would come true. It was going to be a very merry Christmas for all.

L. GODWIN

About the Author

ANN M. MARTIN lives in New York City and loves animals, especially cats. She has two cats of her own, Gussie and Woody.

Other books by Ann M. Martin that you might enjoy are *Stage Fright*; *Me and Katie (the Pest)*; and the books in *The Baby-sitters Club* series.

Ann likes ice cream and *I Love Lucy*. And she has her own little sister, whose name is Jane.

Little Sister

Don't miss #81

KAREN'S ACCIDENT

It was hard to climb down from the tree-house. I forgot that I would have to hold on to the wand. I clutched the wand in one hand and held on to the steps with the other. I looked down. Suddenly the tree house seemed awfully high. I took another step. Oops! My foot slipped. I tried to grab the step above me to hold on, but it was too late. I was already falling.

Bam! I landed on something hard. It was a tree stump sticking out of the snow. Ouch! It had jabbed me right in the side of my stomach. It really hurt. I tried to get up, but it hurt when I moved. So I lay back down in the snow. The magic wand was lying right beside me. Suddenly I did not feel very much like a famous ice skater.

LITTLE APPLE™

BABY SITTERS
Little Sister™

by Ann M. Martin,
author of The Baby-sitters Club ®

More Titles... ➡

Available wherever you buy books, or use this order form.

Scholastic Inc., P.O. Box 7502, 2931 E. McCarty Street, Jefferson City, MO 65102

Please send me the books I have checked above. I am enclosing $ _____
(please add $2.00 to cover shipping and handling). Send check or money order – no
cash or C.O.Ds please.

Name _____ Birthdate _____

Address _____

City _____ State/Zip _____

Please allow four to six weeks for delivery. Offer good in U.S.A. only. Sorry, mail orders are not
available to residents to Canada. Prices subject to change.   BLS5962